The Spider and the Whale

BY LUCY MORONEY

Written by Paul Brown
Illustrated by Rowena Blyth

Spider lived happily
under the warm, snug pipe
in a dark, dusty corner
of the bathroom, spending
the days spinning cobwebs.

Until one fateful day, the owner of the house spotted him!

She let out a horrified scream and flushed poor Spider straight down the toilet!

Immediately, everything went into a spin, and he struggled to keep his head above the strong, swirling water.

Down and down
went Spider through
the dark network
of pipes and sewers.

The torrent of water was so strong,
Spider tumbled over, and over, and over...

...until finally,
the water gushed out
into the sea, belching
out poor little Spider
with it!

He managed to climb aboard a passing pineapple,
and clung on with all his might!

After days and days adrift at sea,
dark storm clouds gathered.

The waves became as big as mountains
and exhausted little Spider had to cling on
tight as the rough sea tossed him up,
down and all around!

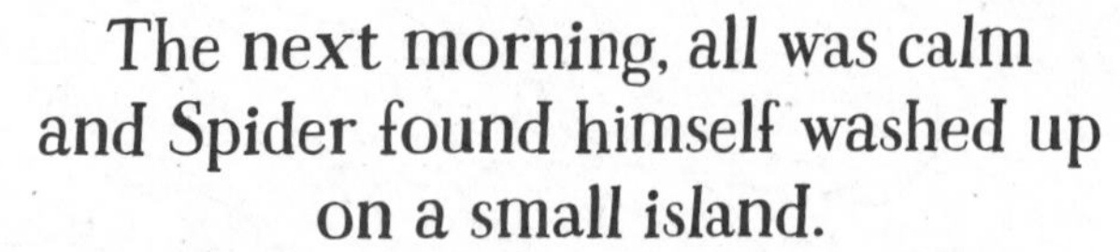

The next morning, all was calm
and Spider found himself washed up
on a small island.

He was safe, but he was so far away from home,
he wondered if he'd ever make it back.
This made Spider so sad, a little tear
ran down his cheek.

"What are you doing on my back?"
asked Whale, a little annoyed.

Spider explained what had happened
and how he needed help to get back home.

Whale liked his new friend and agreed to help
by letting him hitch a ride on his back.

"Thank you for rescuing me Mr Whale.
I promise that one day I will return the favour,"
said Spider.

Then suddenly, something very strange happened! The small island started to slowly move and it squirted up a fountain of water!

But the island
was not an island at all!
It was a ginormous

WHALE!

All the commotion
had woken him from his
long, deep sleep.

"AH, HA, HA, HA!"
laughed mighty Whale.
"What a silly idea."
"I'm so big and strong,
and you're so small and weak–
I don't think I'll ever need your help.
But thank you anyway little Spider".

And so, the two new friends began their journey to find Spider's way back home. Along they travelled through a magnificent, underwater forest of seaweed...

...until they came across a red Lobster who was cutting up greenery for his lunch.

Whale explained to Lobster the promise Spider had made.

Lobster was still laughing to himself as he helped cut a path for Whale and Spider through the dense vegetation.

The three of them journeyed along into the dark depths of the ocean...

...until they bumped into a glowing Jellyfish, who was searching for shiny pearls.

Whale explained to Jellyfish the promise Spider had made.

Jellyfish was still giggling to herself as she lit the way through the darkness for Spider and his friends.

Three became four, and off they journeyed
until they stumbled upon a small
mountain of rocks...

...where they met a burly Octopus who was building a house of boulders.

Whale explained to Octopus the promise Spider had made.

Octopus was still chuckling to himself as he cleared the rocks from the group's path.

Suddenly, out of nowhere,
there was a loud bang
and a huge, heavy net plummeted
down towards them.

Because of his great size,
Whale became entangled in its mesh.

Lobster, Jellyfish and Octopus
were totally frozen by fear, as the
enormous net began hoisting
up their trapped friend!

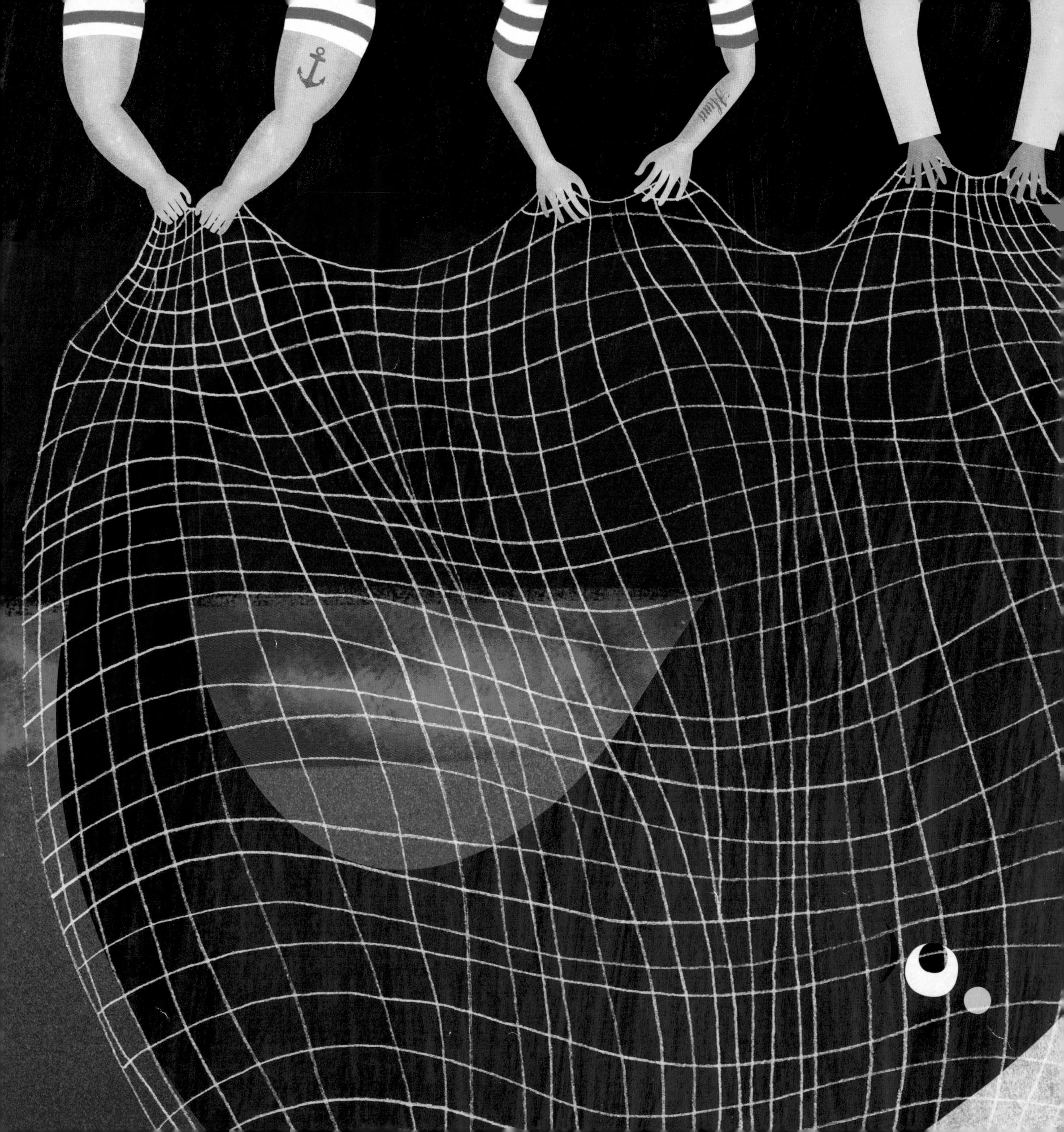
Mum

Even with their combined skills,
the terrified friends could only
look on helplessly as the fishermen
started to haul up their
colossal catch.

Suddenly, little Spider had a fantastic idea, and with no time to lose, he jumped into action!

Spider called out to Octopus
to use his long and plentiful arms
to lift him aboard.
"Mr Lobster, when I give the signal, get ready with your sharp claws," called out Spider.

Once on deck,
Spider climbed onto
a sailor's shoulder
and ever so gently,
tapped his cheek...

The sailor let out
a terrifying shriek
at the sight of Spider.

Then Spider skilfully
jumped from one
shoulder to the next...

...scaring each fisherman
in turn as they let go
of the net in fear!

As soon as the net hit the water,
Spider beckoned Lobster
to cut Whale free.

Quick as a flash,
Spider spun a huge, strong web
to capture the crew so they
could do no more harm.

Whale was finally free and they
were all safe from danger,
as the boat and its bound-up
crew drifted into the distance.

Suddenly, everyone cheered for Spider – the bravest, most heroic one of all!

His quick and clever thinking had saved Whale, and he'd proved that no matter how small you are, you can always be mighty!

"Thank you for saving me Spider.
I will never underestimate you,
or laugh at your size again!"
said Whale.

At that moment, Spider realised his journey was over. He had found a place he could call home with his new-found friends.

And they all celebrated with some delicious jam sandwiches!

ABOUT THE AUTHOR

Schoolgirl, Lucy Moroney lives with her family on the Wirral Peninsula; The Spider and The Whale is her first book.

The story was inspired by an incident in the bathroom when Lucy saw her mummy flush a spider down the toilet!

Lucy's fantastic imagination and her warm sense of humour, helped her create this amusing tale.

In 2017, aged just 9, Lucy was diagnosed with Diffuse Intrinsic Pontine Glioma (DIPG) – a (so far) terminal and inoperable brain tumour.

Proceeds from the sale of this book will go towards Lucy's Pineapple Fund (Lucy really loves pineapples!) to pay for alternative treatments and therapies.

Any additional funds will go towards research into DIPG.

Thank you so much for buying Lucy's book. x

To Maximoo x – L.M.

Thank you to Paul Brown for his assistance with the words and Rowena Blyth for helping with the illustrations.

First published in Great Britain in 2018 by Fourth Wall Publishing

ISBN: 978-1-78749-001-7

www.fourthwallpublishing.com
2 Riverview Business Park, Shore Wood Road, Bromborough, Wirral, Merseyside CH62 3RQ
A catalogue record for this book is available from the British Library
Printed in Bulgaria